Dino-Baby

Mark Sperring

Illustrated by Sam Lloyd

BLOOMSBURY

LONDON NEW DELHI NEW YORK SYDNEY

Do you remember when Dino-Mummy had a tummy bump?

How you placed your head against it
and you heard a little thump?

And can you still remember all the things we said we'd do,
to help our dino-baby be a happy baby-boo?

We said . . .

Be quiet in the morning,
when you first get up . . .

because

thuds

bangs

and

crashes

will wake our dino-pup.

shhhhh!

Don't play rough and tumble
with a little thing like this.

Instead be soft and gentle...

we all LOVE a dino kiss.
MWAAAH!

Don't snatch things away.

And always try to share.

Because when we
play together . . .

it's much more
fun and fair.

A
B
C
Toot! Toot!

Teach our dino-baby all the grown-up things you know...

like saying,

"please"

and

"thank you."

And all the best
places to go.
Whoops!

Show him how to

roar

and

romp,

to clomp
and
stomp
and
pound.

But when it's time for beddy-byes,
say, "Shhhh! Don't make a sound."

And over time, yes day by day,
he'll grow up more and more.

3 metres

2 metres

Until our little
dino-baby...

is a great BIG dinosaur!

Raaah!

For Mandy - MS

For Blake and Mae - SL

Bloomsbury Publishing, London, New Delhi, New York and Sydney
First published in Great Britain in 2013 by Bloomsbury Publishing Plc
50 Bedford Square, London, WC1B 3DP

A CIP catalogue record of this book is available from the British Library

ISBN 978 1 4088 3671 2 (HB)
ISBN 978 1 4088 3672 9 (PB)
ISBN 978 1 4088 3858 7 (eBook)

Printed in China by LEO Paper Product Ltd, HeShan
5 7 9 10 8 6 4

All papers used by Bloomsbury Publishing are natural, recyclable products made from wood grown in well-managed forests. The manufacturing processes conform to the environmental regulations of the country of origin

www.bloomsbury.com